THE CRABIAN HEART

THE CRABIAN HEART

Erik Hofstatter

PARALLEL UNIVERSE PUBLICATIONS

ISBN: 9780995717367
Parallel Universe Publications, 130 Union Road,
Oswaldtwistle, Lancashire, BB5 3DR, UK

CONTENTS

INTRODUCTION TO THE CRABIAN HEART
Karen Runge

One of the most stunning aspects of the horror genre, to anyone who takes the time to notice, is its capacity for tenderness. *Tenderness?* some would gasp at this statement. *Blood? Guts? Death, betrayal, murder, violence, gore, and wretched, soul-torn helplessness... is* tender? *No way!* Oh, but it is. And it couldn't be any other way, because without love, empathy, insight, concern, hope, heroics, compassion... the very trappings that give any feeling heart the capacity to hurt... horror just doesn't work. Why would it matter to you that someone's world is ripped to shreds and they are forced onto the darkest of journeys, if you didn't feel for that person? If it didn't on some level, however vicarious, matter to you that these terrible things are happening to someone you hold dear, even if only as a character on the page or screen? There are a lot of contradictions in the ways horror works. But within those contradictions there is a genuine, soul-deep sincerity that rips the truest, brightest pattern through each and every story it tells. Pain has the power to move, just as much as beauty does. And the contradictory symmetry of horror works in a way that, when you notice it and learn how to read it, can be astonishingly, paralyzingly beautiful.

Which brings me to the works of Erik Hofstatter. Schlock horror is a thing apart from horror's other (admittedly, incredibly broad) other sub-genres. William Peter Blatty's *The Exorcist* is often mistaken for Schlock (spinning heads? masturbation with crucifixes?) but is so finely written and so emotionally intuitive that it really stands, on closer inspection, as one of the most overlooked literary masterpieces of recent times. (A certain young lady who produced her own vicious masterpiece back in the Victorian era would likely relate to this same problem with people's perceptions of her work.) Brian Keene's much more recent sex-guts-depravity tale *The Ghoul* is described as Schlock, and (as far as I can tell) in fact actually is. So, what then is the difference between what we might (very reluctantly in too many cases) describe as *literary* horror, and what we broadstroke as *Schlock* horror?

Here's a little personal tale that set the mark for my tastes as a horror fan, and which captures this exact question with that very magical symmetry I'm trying to define. When I was twelve years old, my older brother would sneak out the house at night to meet with his friends and cause their own little level of harmless mayhem upon the streets of our very sleepy rural hometown. This was standard order where we grew up—the nearest city was a very perilous mountain-pass hour away by car, and our town's desperately bored teenagers didn't have much else to do to entertain themselves except bust out their houses at night and get up to mischief whilst their parents slept unawares. As 'little sister', and still too young to join my brother on these, ahem, rip-wild late night excursions, it was my job to stay up watching TV and cover for my rebel bro while he got up to all sorts of what-the-fuck-ever in the tiny streets and surrounding woods with his weed-smoking, car-'borrowing' friends. I was a good little sister, always ready to stand duty, dreaming of the days my brother would hold out his hand for me as he climbed out his bedroom window and say, 'Come with me.' So what did I do, while he and the cool kids got up to all sorts and I sat in my pink (okay, like I would *ever* really wear pink...) jammies, all posed to reassure our mother and send her back to bed if she came to check on us? I watched movies. Good old M-Net, which only fellow South Africans close to my age would even know about, was the only channel that showed ad-free films late at night, age-restricted films included. Did I mention that this particular night was Halloween? No? Well....

Halloween movie night marathon, here I come, solo, keeping one ear out for my mother's footsteps coming down the passage (1. She's going to walk in during some gory/sexy scene and say WHAT THE HELL ARE YOU WATCHING OMIGOD GO TO BED, or 2. She's going to say WHAT THE HELL ARE YOU WATCHING OMIGOD AND WHERE THE HELL IS YOUR BROTHER??) and the other ear out for my beloved older bro scrabbling his drunk/stoned/probably both ass back in through his bedroom window. It's okay. Mom's asleep, I've got a mug of hot chocolate and a bunch of comfy pillows. Let's do this thing. First in the line-up: *Tales from the Crypt: Demon Knight*. Followed by: *The Crow*.

Hear me, please. I already knew I was a horror fan. Really, I did. But I was twelve years old, and as far as I knew horror went no further than R.L. Stine and a (very barely remembered) attempt at watching a greasy copy of *Predator* on VHS. (Yeah... I'm that old. Let's not get into that.) So this first film was unlike anything I'd ever seen. I had no idea that fists could bust all the motherfucking way through skulls (yes yes I know they can't but jayzum crow that looked real!!) and I had no idea that demons could dream of love, or that green slime could birth head-banded beasties or that... or that...!!! Yep. That was my introduction to Schlock. I couldn't wait for my brother to come back so I could make him feel awful about all the cool shit I'd just seen, that he'd just missed out on because he'd rather, I dunno, hang out with girls and smoke weed over hanging with his little sister and seeing this... this...

When *Demon Knight* was done the world had already tilted on its axis. I was a freaking livewire. Not only had I never seen anything so cool in my little life before, but the very idea that such amazingly cool stuff even existed was like something from another realm for me.

But we're not done yet. Here comes Halloween Fest movie #2. *The Crow.*

As famous as it already was, growing up where I did, I had no idea about it. When I eventually left this little town at 18, I was astonished to discover that *The Crow* stands as a cult classic smash hit. (No, I *really* didn't know. Stop judging please.) I'm now a proud owner of the graphic novel, and again, like much of my horror genre mania, I owe my passion for it to that night. Because that night I thought I was covering for my brother, and happy to do so because of my open interest in horror. But really what I was doing was getting a four-hour crash-course in just how far and wide the horror genre reaches.

Fast-forward a few years (no, I will not divulge exactly how many I mean by a 'few'...) and I've gone full hardcore horror fan, to the point where I create horror-inspired visual art and write my own short stories and books. On this journey of establishing myself as a horror artist in my own right, I got to know a few amazing fellow fans and creators. While my own horror fiction is often more serious (more *The Crow* than *Demon Knight*, for example) I've always been a staunch defender of Schlock and all its other many sub-genres. One of these people I've got to know of course would have to be Erik Hofstatter, the mad genius of Schlock who I think everyone with half a heart for horror *really really needs to read.* I acted as first-run editor on a couple of his earlier published works, and the first time I got the style of his work, I thought... *This is like something from Tales from the Crypt.* And thought back immediately to that fateful cushion-hugging night I spent as a pre-teen so many (but not *that* many!) moons ago.

Erik's work is special in that while it's easy to compare the feel of his art to *Tales from the Crypt,* there's a fair bit of *The Crow* in there too. Erik writes Schlock with more depth than many of the big names in the sub-genre could come close to claiming. He's like a tight-rope walker, perfectly balanced between raucous, hellacious gore-fest and deeply sensitive, soul-tweaking depths.

In this work, *The Crabian Heart,* Erik takes a few steps away from pure Schlock and nestles a little closer to the empathetic depths that make his particular brand so very special. There may not be much gore in this particular tale of his, but you won't really notice. Because less *Demon Knight* and more *The Crow,* what he measures out here instead is built on a carefully-carved empathy, echoed back and mirrored for you in many of its most fragile forms. Horror doesn't work without love. And this story is all about love. Which is exactly what makes it all about horror.

To the demons both within and without, dear reader. Green-slime covered or otherwise. There's a heart beating in here. Enjoy it.

Karen Runge, November 2017

THE CRABIAN HEART

E-N-O-L-A
A-L-O-N-E

"Where is Dad? What have they done with him?"

Irena dropped her rucksack like an anchor and faced the miserable building. Like her, it had seen better years. She slumped against the patch of chipped facade. Her trapezius muscle burned from the added weight of despair.

"I told you where he is. In prison. They locked him up. It's just us for now."

Aleš gazed at their earthly belongings, orphaned beneath his mother's feet. "But why?"

"I don't know why. It's just something that they do—it's like a part of their process or something."

She rubbed her screaming neck with sore fingers.

"For how long?"

"For as long as it takes. Now gimme a hand with this thing."

The boy hesitated. "But where are we going to sleep?"

"Here for now. The East Cliff Hotel. Our new home," she said, her tone masking a mild disappointment. Irena studied the red phone box by the entrance — an icon of English culture. A misshapen plant was dying inside.

"Why put a tree in a phone booth?" Aleš said.

Irena shrugged. "It's for decorative purposes."

"The tree?"

"No, the phone box. It's a replica — it doesn't work."

Seagulls screeched like winged beggars and the boy's eyes leaked excitement. "Listen! That means there's sea nearby. Where is it? Where is the sea? You promised me a sea."

Irena flung the rucksack back over her shoulder, a sigh of defeat almost spilled from her cracked lips. "I know. You shall have it, but not just yet."

"I've never seen a sea before," Aleš said.

She mustered a weak nod. "Neither have I."

Growing silence wedged them apart and they blinked in unison.

"Are you hungry?" Irena said.

The boy swallowed a wave of salty air. "Yes."

"Okay. Come on then; hopefully they'll feed us. We can look for the sea tomorrow."

They shuffled inside. The White Cliffs of Dover towered above like sleeping chalk giants.

*

The lobby smelled of mothballs and foreign accents. Irena sank into an embroiled sofa, her fingers circling a hole in the cushion. She pinched the stuffing in blind frustration.

"What now?" Aleš said.

She grimaced at the peeling wallpaper. The entire décor invited depression.

"We wait."

"For what?"

Irena massaged the bridge of her nose. "For someone to notice us."

Aleš groaned. "I'm hungry."

"We both are. Look, that woman is waving at me. She must be our point of contact. Stay here while I talk to her."

The boy watched as the elderly woman strolled towards them with melodic footsteps. She seemed odd in her mismatched clothes, short cropped hair, and pink scarf. Her generous smile was contradicted by her greedy eyes. The eyes of a gypsy.

"Hellooooo. My name is Zsófia. Welcome to East Cliff. Or welcome to England I should say."

Her handshake was cold and feeble. Irena also registered a speck of accent, not dissimilar to her own.

"Thank you. I'm Irena and that's my son, Aleš."

Zsófia narrowed her eyes and fished in her pockets like an autistic magician. She produced a half melted Milky Way bar and tossed it to him. Aleš caught the chocolate in cupped palms, his face projecting gratitude in a thousand dead languages.

Irena pursed her lips, offering a tired smile. "So what do we do now? They gave us this map when we arrived and told us to come here."

"Yes, yes. Do not worry. Everything has been

taken care of for the duration of your application. You will receive a weekly allowance for food and basic hygiene necessities. Your room is ready, too." She produced a tattered card. "You have an appointment at 10 am tomorrow morning. The address is on the card, but it's literally just over the road. They'll explain in more detail what's likely to happen. Your husband's been detained, I take it?"

Irena's jaw was clenched, and her eyes burned like a dying comet. Zsófia squeezed her hand in rehearsed sympathy.

"I'm sorry, dear. They do that to all arriving families—detain the fathers, I mean. Your husband will be fine. Where are you from, if you don't mind my asking?"

"The Czech Republic," Irena said, choosing not to elaborate.

"Ah, yes. Hungarian blood flows in my veins so we're practically neighbours, but enough of my prattling. Let me show you to your room."

The gypsy ushered them past a fruit machine and upstairs onto the second floor. She paused and pivoted on the bottom stair. "Here are your keys. This one is to the front door and this one to your room. The front entrance stays open during the day, but we lockdown at 22:00."

Irena slipped the keys inside her back pocket. "Thanks. What about the food situation?"

"I'll fix you something for tonight and for tomorrow morning," Zsófia said, grasping the rail as they ascended. "Once you collect your allowance, you'll be responsible for your own meals. There is a small kitchenette you can use. I'll show you tomorrow."

Aleš peered at the railing, noticing cracks and chips in the white paint. The empty walls leered at him, or so he thought.

"And here we are. Please go in and make yourselves comfortable. I'll send up two plates of beans on toast in half an hour. We'll have a proper chat tomorrow when you're both rested. It's been a long day, I'm sure. Good night."

They thanked her. The room looked like something out of a Hitchcock film. Aleš pounced on the mattress, watching his mother fiddle with the lock.

"What do you think?" Irena said.

"About what?"

"The room…"

His eyes found a small telly, tucked in a corner. "There's no VCR."

"We'll get you one, once we're settled in."

Aleš nodded and curled into a human ball. "Maybe we can ask her?"

"Who? That Zsófia person? Don't be silly."

"Why not?"

"The way she looked at us," Irena said, unfastening her rucksack, "like we were insects, crawling from some dilapidated shack."

"But she smiled the whole time."

Irena slipped her blouse onto the plastic hanger. "Her smile was thinner than a razorblade. And her eyes. It's all in the eyes. They never lie, no matter how pleasant you pretend to be."

"What do you mean?"

"Well, some people are like an open book—you just have to know how to read them."

"Okay."

Irena read him now. He understood nothing.

"What's the matter?"

"I miss Dad," Aleš said.

She cuddled her son and breathed in the musky scent of his hair. "I miss him, too."

"When can we see him?"

"I don't know, hopefully soon."

"He didn't do anything wrong."

"I know," she said.

"Are we safe?"

"For the time being, yes."

"They won't find us?"

"I don't think so."

"Okay."

She patted his shoulder. "Now let's see if we can find you some Van Damme on the telly while we wait for our meal."

Aleš whooped and for a second her life made sense again.

*

Humdrum cars swirled a roundabout and Irena hesitated. The alien traffic system baffled her. Their bellies were filled with cheesy omelettes and cheap coffee. Aleš pointed to the other side. "That's where the sea is. She said so."

Irena followed his finger, eyes watery from the brash daylight. "Okay. We'll take a stroll after our appointment."

"I want to go now," Aleš said.

Irena glanced at her vintage Oris watch. "We gotta be there in ten minutes. They won't like it if we're late."

"I don't want to see them. You go and I'll meet you back at the hotel."

"Aleš, don't be ridiculous. We're in a foreign country. You'll get lost and then what?"

He fiddled in his pockets, as if searching for some persuasion totem. "How can I get lost? The sea is *right* there. Please?"

She groaned, her mind sliced into two. "Fine. But don't do anything idiotic."

"Like what?"

"Like talk to strangers, fall into the sea, get mowed by a car, that sort of thing?"

"Okay."

"Don't make me regret this. When you're done with the sea, return straight to the hotel. Promise? I'll be back in an hour or so."

"Okay."

She checked her watch again. Her shoulders twitched with something like impatience. "No, promise me."

"I promise."

"Good. I'll see you in a bit."

The boy waved goodbye and pressed the pedestrian crossing button, another oddity he had never seen before. Illuminated letters spelled WAIT. He did.

*

Aleš trailed the seagull's song—a symphony of screeching hunger. The darkened sky was smeared with abandoned hope. And then he gasped. Ocean. An actual ocean. Right there in front of him. He guzzled sporadic waves with his eyes and imagined myriads of secrets beneath them, floating. The colour confused him. He expected blue, but it was poisoned with something else.

"It changed its colour again. Like a chameleon."

A frail girl stood next to him. Her face was pale and impassive. She wore a knitted jumper that was too big for her skinny frame.

"Why is it purple?" Aleš said.

She shrugged. "Dunno. Our sea is strange. Always has been."

"I've never seen a sea before."

"How disappointed you must be."

Her sonorous voice betrayed a hidden maturity, as if she was privy to humanity's true purpose.

"What's your name?"

"Enola."

"I'm Aleš," he said, extending his right hand.

"I can't shake your *right* hand."

He retracted it, sheepish. "You don't shake hands in this country?"

"We do."

"Okay."

Then he realised what she meant. The right sleeve of her jumper hung flaccid, empty.

"How old are you?"

"T-t-thirteen," he stammered, still shocked by the absence of her arm.

Enola tilted her head, surveying him with eyes that seemed older than the sea. Greasy black curls spilled down her spine.

"Are you scared of me?"

"No, why would I be?" he said, inflating his chest.

"Because I'm different. People are scared of what they don't know…or understand."

Her skin was besmirched with dirt and Aleš wondered when she last bathed.

"You look tired."

"I am," she said, the shadows beneath her eyes now prominent.

Aleš directed his gaze towards the purple waves. They sparkled like fading promises of youth.

"Walk with me."

"Where?"

"Along the shore," Enola said.

"Okay."

They leapt off the promenade path and into the crunching pebbles below. Aleš waddled but she strolled beside him with patient grace.

"Where do you live?"

"Nearby," she said.

"Okay. How old are you?"

Enola paused and scooped a fistful of smooth stones. "Thirteen. More or less."

"What do you mean?"

She tossed the stones into the sea, one by one. Her eyes were closed, as if she was counting wishes, but her shoulder was unnaturally stiff. Each pebble she threw twisted her face with pain.

"Why did you come here?"

"Because I wanted to see the ocean," he said.

"No. Why did you come to England?"

"How did you—"

"Your accent…"

"Oh," Aleš said, scratching his temple.

"Well?"

"Better life, I guess."

Enola scoffed. "There's nothing *better* about life here."

The sea gurgled in agreement.

"You sound like you hate life."

"I do."

"Why?"

Her gaze grew distant then.

"You'd hate life too if your body was locking up."

"What do you mean?"

"It doesn't matter."

Aleš buried his trainer into the pebbles, sweeping.

"Do you want to search for fossils?"

"No."

"Okay."

He ran to a maze of chalk boulders five metres ahead. In his peripheral vision, he registered movement. Aleš crouched and spotted a small, purple crab hiding in a shade. Its pincers reached out to him like a drowning child.

"Don't touch it. They are not what they seem."

Aleš veered, baffled. Her face was stiff, like the rest of her body.

"What do you mean? And how did you get here so fast? I didn't hear you."

Enola shivered, from cold or anger — he could not tell.

"I think you should go home now. And stay away from the crabs."

*

The fruit machine's hypnotic lights lured him in. Aleš tapped on the play button, seduced, but the rotating reels ignored him.

"You have to feed it coins, young man."

Aleš veered and blinked at the gypsy. "Why?"

"It's a game of chance, much like your life."

"What do you mean?"

She swung her arm around his shoulder. "Never mind. You're too young to gamble. What would your mother think, eh?"

Aleš blushed.

"Don't worry. I'll keep your secret, if you promise to keep mine."

"What's your secret?"

Zsófia peered down at him with muddled eyes. The atmosphere grew thinner.

"I play sometimes. Late at night, when no-one's watching," she whispered.

A sudden shock replaced his smile when he met her gaze. Pellets of purple filled her irises. He flinched.

"Fancy some tea?"

"Okay."

She led him into a cluttered dining room.

"Take a seat and I'll be right back."

Aleš obeyed and thought about Enola. He missed her already. She was an enigma, something dangerous but exhilarating—like diving with sharks. Her company dulled the pain of existence.

"Here we are, plenty of milk and three sugars."

"Thank you," he said, watching steam dance with the cup.

Zsófia joined him behind the table and stirred her tea with a spoon of questionable origins.

"Did you manage to find the beach?"

"Yes, thank you."

"Was it nice?"

"Yes," Aleš said, blowing on his tea.

"What did your mother think?"

"I went alone."

"Oh, how come?"

"She had an appointment with *them*."

Zsófia tapped her forehead. "Of course! I forgot. How silly of me."

"It's okay. The sea confused me, though."

"The sea? Why?"

"It was purple, not blue."

She cackled. "Purple? That's…interesting."

"It was! My friend saw it, too."

"I believe you. What's her name?"

"Enola. Wait—how did you know it was a girl?"

"Lucky guess. Do you like her?"

"I think so," he said, sheepish.

"Is she pretty?"

Aleš nodded, then hesitated. "Well, I dunno. She's a bit strange."

"In what way?"

"I dunno, like she's different to the girls I went to school with. She looks kinda stiff and smells funny."

The gypsy swallowed a mouthful of tea. "You're a stranger in a strange land, lad. It will take time to acclimatize yourself, but make no mistake—cultural differences can be challenging."

"Okay."

"What else did you get up to?"

"We found a crab, but she told me to stay away from it."

Zsófia offered him a biscuit. "Smart girl. It's best not to meddle with nature."

As she passed him the bowl, he spotted asymmetrical cuts and bruises on her inner forearm. They were purple, like the sea, like her eyes.

"What happened to your arm?"

She rolled her sleeve down, head shaking. "I'm a silly old woman. I slipped on the stairs and landed on my arm. It's not as bad as it looks."

"Okay."

"Finish your tea, lad, and check on your mother. She should be back by now."

*

Inside the room, Irena paced side to side like a human pendulum. She grimaced.

"What's that?"

"A map," she said, handing it to him.

Aleš peered at the photocopied sheet. A route was highlighted in fluorescent yellow. He navigated with his finger along the smudged street names.

"To where?"

"A building where we get our allowance from."

"Is it far?"

She snatched the paper from him and folded it into a little rectangle.

"They said about twenty minutes tops. Come on then."

Aleš groaned. "Do I have to? I'd rather go to the beach."

"What? You just came back."

"I know, but I like it there."

She grabbed her purse off the bed. "Well, it's your choice. You can come to town with me, or you can go to the beach and eat pebbles for lunch."

The oncoming traffic slithered like mechanical snails.

"Look, we're moving faster than them."

Irena pressed his arm down. "Don't point."

"Why are they driving on the wrong side of the road?"

"Burns less petrol."

"Really?"

"No. Come on, silly. We haven't got all day."

"Okay."

They veered right, strolling past a leisure centre that begged for renovation. Irena paused, fishing the map out from her purse.

"According to this, there should be a market square at the end of the road. Look for a fountain."

"Okay," Aleš said, nodding.

He followed his mother's lead. The cobblestones were smeared with dry phlegm and his stomach somersaulted. Then he glimpsed jets of water in the distance.

"That must be the fountain," he said, pointing at the raised podium.

"Well done, Sherlock."

Aleš battled the urge to splash his mother while Irena studied the map again—head rotating left and right.

"Do you see that blue sign over there? That must be the place. Let's go."

"Government buildings are boring."

"So?"

"Can I stay here?"

She clenched her fist and her jaw muscles tightened. "You enjoy abandoning me, don't you? Fine. But stay close to the fountain, you hear me?"

"I will, don't worry."

"I'm just gonna fill in some paperwork and hopefully collect our food money—be back in a jiffy."

"Okay."

Aleš kneeled at the base and karate-chopped streams of gushing water. The rustling bubbles drowned his mother's mumbles. As he dunked his fingers, the liquid blushed with a tint of purple and he spotted a crab-like shape sprawled on the mosaic tiles. The crustacean signalled with its right pincer in a continuous jabbing motion. His eyes scanned the pointed direction and he glimpsed the familiar silhouette of the girl. He mouthed her name, but she was too far to hear. When he lowered his gaze, the water was clear again and the creature gone.

"What are you doing?"

He recognised the voice of his mother. "Thought I saw something."

"I bet people throw all kinds of weird junk down there. You hungry?"

"Starving," Aleš said.

"We're in luck. There's a burger joint over there, look."

"Can I have a cheeseburger?"

"No, but you can have a double."

*

A swarm of noisy immigrants congregated in the reception when they returned. Zsófia greeted them with a semi-circular smile, her manners rehearsed to perfection. Irena wiggled her nose and shifted towards the stairwell.

"Wait, wait. Did you get it sorted?"

Aleš shrugged his shoulders, hands filled with plastic shopping bags.

"Yes, thank you. We bought some food, as you can see, so should be good for now," Irena said.

The gypsy nodded like a circus seal. "Excellent. Well, if you need anything else just let me know."

"Thanks. You're clearly busy so don't worry about us."

Irena nudged the door with her robust arse and they disappeared into a meagre kitchenette. Aleš practised his Karate kicks while she filled cupboards with canned goods.

"So what happens to us now? When can we visit Dad?"

"I don't know. I have another appointment next week."

"Okay."

"For now, we just have to focus on settling in and finding our routine."

"Are you gonna get a job?" Aleš said.

"I can't."

"Why?"

She inspected the fridge and scoffed. "Look at the state of it."

"Why can't you get a job?"

"I'm not allowed."

"What about me?"

"You're too young to get a job," she said, soaking a cloth in the sink.

"No, I meant will they put me in school?"

"I don't know, Aleš. Everything's uncertain. I don't know how it all works."

"Okay. Can I go to the beach?"

"Tomorrow?"

"Now."

"Once a day is enough, don't you think?"

He shook his head.

"It's already getting dark out there."

"Only for a little while, I promise."

Irena sighed and closed the fridge. "You're persistent like your father. Go if you must. But be back in an hour, you hear me?"

"Okay."

"What are you doing there anyway?"

"I listen to the sea."

"You'd rather listen to the sea than your old mum, huh? I get that. Off you go then. Have fun."

Aleš thanked her and sprinted back to the reception. The gypsy lingered by the door and he wondered if she was eavesdropping.

"No running in the hotel, young man. Where you're going at this hour?"

"To the beach."

Zsófia lowered her voice. "A late date, is it?"

"No..." he said, eyes glued to his trainers.

"Your secret is safe with me, don't you worry."

"I just fancied a stroll on the beach."

"The sea speaks many languages..."

"It speaks to you, too?" Aleš said.

She pressed a finger to her lips. "Shush. That's between us."

"Okay."

"Our sea is potent, you know?"

He nodded.

"Do you believe me?"

"It's the only sea I've ever seen."

"And the only one worth seeing."

Aleš wondered what she meant by that.

"Apologies for rambling. Don't keep the lady waiting."

"I don't even know if she'll be there..."

The gypsy narrowed her eyes. "She doesn't know you're coming?"

"No. I was just hoping she might turn up."

"She'll be there, trust me."

"Okay."

He grinned and turned to the exit.

"Aleš?"

"Yes?"

"If you want to keep your love safe—stay away from the crabs."

*

The promenade was sprayed with quiet melancholy.

Aleš sloped against the ghost white railings, his eyes peeled on foggy outlines of faraway ferries, sailing into grey. A rustling sound behind him eradicated his reverie. When he veered, a skeletal seagull was devouring fish remains from a dented bin. The primal act of survival filled him with gratitude, for his mother and adoptive country. Scavenging was a frightening prospect. He hopped of the sea wall, seeking refuge from an invasive current of wind that kept rearranging his hairstyle.

"Hello."

Aleš landed on a cocktail of pebbles and right next to her. She was alone, hugging her knees.

"Whoa. I didn't see you there. I could've crushed you."

"I don't think so."

"What are you doing here? Sitting all by yourself."

"The same as you—I'm listening to the sea," Enola said.

He crouched, tucking in shoelaces. "Was that you earlier? In town?"

"What?"

"I saw you in town earlier, at least I think it was you."

"Where?"

"By the fountain. There was this crab—"

Her voice mutated then, as if a storm brewed inside her throat. "I told you to stay away from them."

"I tried, but the crab was just *there*. I couldn't help it."

"No contact?"

"What do you mean?"

Enola inhaled, louder than necessary. "Did you touch it?"

"No," Aleš said.

"Good. Stay away from them."

"You sound like Zsófia."

"Who?"

He lost balance and toppled over on his buttocks. "Ouch. This old woman we're staying with. She owns the hotel."

"You like her?"

Aleš thought about it. "No, she's kind of creepy."

"Why?"

"Her eyes turned purple the other day and she has these purple bruises on her arm."

"Maybe she came from the sea," Enola said.

"Why would she come from the sea?"

"That's where the crabs come from…"

Aleš chuckled. "But she's not a crab, stupid."

"You're right," she said.

"Have you sat here long?"

"A while."

"Are you cold?"

"No."

"Come on, let's have a throwing contest."

"What?"

"We'll each take a pebble and see who can throw it farthest into the sea."

"No."

Aleš curled his bottom lip. "You can't throw with your left?"

"I can, but I'm weak."

He squeezed her arm and recoiled in shock.

"Don't do that," Enola said.

"It's so stiff…I can't feel any muscle."

"I'm a girl, I'm not supposed to have muscles."

"Yeah, but—"

"No buts. It's better for you if you don't touch me."

"Okay."

"How long will you stay in that hotel?"

"I don't know," Aleš said, biting his nails. "Our application can take weeks, months, even years."

"Is that what your mum said?"

He nodded.

"I'm here for you, if you need me."

"Thanks, but you don't exactly understand my situation."

"And you don't understand mine," Enola said with moist eyes.

"Please don't cry…"

"Why?"

"I don't like it when you're upset."

"Do you care about me?"

Aleš nodded again, words barricaded behind his tongue.

"I can't *love* you."

Something in her tone speared his heart. "Why not?"

"I just can't."

"Okay."

"Can you bring me that purple little rock over there?"

"What, the one way down there?"

She tilted her head, sadness spreading in her eyes like cancer. "Yes."

"Okay."

The sea whispered, and strands of slimy seaweed fettered around his ankles as he waddled down the beach. Still eyes of crabs lurked between stones. Enola devoured his every step. Then she vanished.

*

Aleš wandered to the hotel ten minutes after his curfew. Deformed shadows hung from walls in the dimply-lit reception. Earlier chaos was replaced with fractured serenity. Zsófia relaxed on a moth-eaten sofa, knitting.

"What's the matter, lad? You seem troubled."

He smudged his tears with a knuckle. "She just left me there, alone on the beach—didn't even say goodbye."

"Come here, sit with me."

"She said she couldn't love me."

Zsófia stopped knitting and dropped purple needles into her lap. "Love is unpredictable, just like the sea."

"I hate love. Wish I didn't feel it."

"Yes, I had the same wish once."

"What do you mean?" Aleš said.

The wrinkled corner of her mouth stretched into a nostalgic smile. "To be immune to love."

"Okay," he blinked, confused but intrigued.

"Want me to tell you a little story?"

"Okay."

"It's a sad tale, I'm afraid. Perhaps best not to relay it now."

"Please, I want to hear it."

The gypsy sighed and readjusted her cushion. "Very well. I was married once, long time ago. We happened to be on the same ferry, sailing from Calais to Dover. He was a charismatic man. Broad shoulders, olive complexion, hypnotic eyes. I melted like a candle when I saw him. He sensed my infatuation and approached me. We flirted and began dating shortly after. We bought this hotel together, you know?"

Aleš nodded, listening. "Love at first sight?"

"Yes, I suppose. Sounds silly now. I loved him unequivocally and showered him with devotion. We had a blissful life and never struggled for money. Our conversations were epic. It was beautiful, cleansing. Years drifted by and we grew stronger. Us against the world, that was my philosophy. But my heart was pure, naïve. And then he crushed it."

"How?"

"He was seeing someone else. For months. A cliché, I know, but I was blinded by love. Never saw it coming. Struck me like thunder on a moonless night. Still, his infidelity was unorthodox you may say."

"What do you mean?" Aleš said.

She crossed her legs. "Well, his betrayal wasn't sexual."

"What kind of other betrayal is there?"

"*Emotional*, which is far more severe."

"I don't get it."

Zsófia flashed her stained teeth. "Yes, you're far too young to understand. But my tale is a valuable lesson for you. Heed my words."

"Okay. Did you leave him in the end?"

"No, he was noble enough to leave *me*."

"Hmm, maybe you could've fixed it?"

"Forgiveness doesn't come easily to me, lad. When you invest your heart and soul only to be betrayed, well—it *changes* you."

"But some marriages survive worse, no?"

"Some do, yes, but I didn't want to live a lie. A broken trust leaves a nasty scar. Perhaps our marriage could have been healed, but that scar would be visible on the surface—always."

Aleš pondered her words. "Did you ever marry again?"

"No. I did not possess the strength or courage."

"That is kind of sad…"

"It certainly is. I wandered the beach for hours, drowning in despair. I prayed to the sea to take me and end my pain."

"Did it answer your prayers?"

"Yes, a crab appeared on the shore."

"A crab?"

"Yes. Do you remember when I told you to stay away from them, if you want to keep your love safe?"

He nodded.

"The crabs possess a unique ability. A gift to some, a curse to others."

"What ability?"

"They can—"

Irena barged into the reception, her breath hectic. "There you are! I told you to be home half an hour ago. I was so worried."

Aleš bit his lower lip in panic.

"I'm so sorry, it's my fault. Please forgive me," Zsófia said, stumbling to her feet.

"What's going on?"

The boy turned to his mother. "She was telling me a story. We're not finished."

"Oh, yes you are. Dinner's ready."

"I'll tell you the rest some other time, don't you worry. Off you go, lad. Listen to your mother."

"Thank you," Irena said, dragging him out of the hall.

*

"What exactly was she telling you?"

"Just a story," he said, sprinkling parmesan on his spag bol.

"Stay away from her. I don't like the way she looks at you."

"What do you mean?"

"I mean what I said. Avoid her, you hear me?"

"But we *live* here," Aleš said.

"Yes, I'm aware of that."

"How can I avoid her then?"

Irena rubbed her forehead until the skin turned pink. "I spoke to a woman yesterday; an immigrant like us."

"About what?"

"About our situation and what to expect. This accommodation is only temporary, a week or two max."

"Okay. What happens after?"

"They'll relocate us to a flat of our own. All expenses paid for."

"For how long?"

"Until our application is reviewed and a decision is made. We're talking months and months."

"Okay."

"How do you feel about that?"

Aleš guillotined his pasta with a crooked fork. "Would we stay in Dover?"

"I'm sorry, darling, but that seems unlikely."

"But I have a friend here."

"That old woman?"

"No, someone else."

Irena furrowed her brows. "Who?"

"I started talking to a girl on the beach. She's nice."

Irena ruffled his hair from across the table. "A girl, eh? That's why you're so obsessed with the beach. I'm sorry, but it's out of my hands. We don't get a say. We've got to go where they tell us to go."

"Why?"

"Because they make the rules."

"Okay."

"Better not get too attached to this girl, right?"

"I can't choose who I fall in love with," he said.

"Aleš, please. We have bigger things to worry about. You can hang out with her for a few more days, but be ready—they'll move us soon. Or worse."

"What do you mean?"

"Don't think of it now. Are you finished?"

A ball of spaghetti was curled on his plate like incestuous worms. His appetite diminished.

"Stop poking it around. Brush your teeth and off to bed with you. I'll be up in a minute."

*

On the edge of the shore she waited for him. The tide was low and purple waves chastised her feet. She faced him, beckoning with a smile that promised eternity. Her hair shone in the dying light. The right sleeve of her transparent nightgown was no longer flaccid. She seemed restored, seraphic. Aleš bathed in the thinly veiled form of her still-developing body. His fingers ached with desire to hold and touch her, to inhale the intoxicating perfume of her skin. She sheltered him from a damaged world. He found acceptance in her embrace. She was his portal to instant happiness. A myriad of possibilities swam around him, but he only wanted her. To battle each day by her side.

Together. The festering disease of their reality nothing but a crippled memory. Soon. A circle of seagulls bore witness to their union. They sang, lamenting lost souls. The kingdom was near. Hidden, sleepless. She called his name and the sound of her voice carried him forward. Wind cooled his cheeks.

He drew closer, drunk on illusions, but the sea stirred with his steps. The sky warped. Waves gurgled, and a darkling shape broke the surface. Aleš gasped, heart throbbing in his chest. The figure wore a human face, Zsófia's face, but her entire body was engulfed with crabs. She towered over Enola, leering with destruction. Thousands of pincers clicked in unison, demanding flesh.

She reeked of broken love. He wanted to scream, to warn Enola, but words refused to form. Zsófia embraced her, tighter and tighter, legions of crustaceans marching from her body to Enola's. The mother of crabs whispered into her ear, uttering words from a long-forgotten language. Enola surrendered, one of the children slid inside her mouth, and more burrowed into her skin. Then Zsófia yanked her beneath the waves as he watched in impotent horror. She gloated, singing hymns from the darkest depths. Aleš sobbed on the shore, his tears purple as the sea. Alone.

*

The boy panicked, drenched in sweat, and his pulse racing. He rolled out of bed, thirsty. Irena was asleep, her chest rising in a steady rhythm, her pleasant dreams mocking his nightmare. A bottle of mineral water hid in the cupboard and he gulped it down like a suffocating carp.

"What are you doing up so early?" Irena said, yawning and cracking her fingers.

"I have to see her."

"See who?"

"Enola."

"The girl from the beach?"

Aleš nodded, screwing the plastic cap back on.

"No need to rush."

"I had a bad dream, I want to make sure she's all right."

"Eat some breakfast first," she said, but Aleš ignored her.

"I will later."

"Fine. Take an apple with you at least and be back in an hour, okay?"

"Okay."

*

Voices quadrupled in the lounge. Aleš observed a shambolic arrival of a new Syrian family. Gratitude burned bright in their fatigued faces. A familiar figure protruded behind them. He tilted his head. Enola gazed at the fruit machine, her neck and shoulders stiff, like a human statue. She seemed out of place.

"You don't belong here," Aleš said.

She turned her head to meet his eyes, but he saw only pain.

"What's wrong?"

"My muscles…"

"What about your muscles?"

"They're turning into bone."

Aleš blinked, perplexed. "What do you mean?"

"I came here to warn you."

"Warn me? About what?"

"That woman you told me about. She wants your heart. Or what's inside it," Enola said.

"I don't understand. What are you talking about? And why did you leave me last time?"

The flashing lights recaptured her attention. Her expression was strange, as if she contemplated gambling her life. Like she had nothing else to lose.

"I had to go."

"Why?"

"I was summoned."

Aleš scratched his ear. "I don't know what summoned means."

"I was called."

"Okay. But you should've said goodbye."

"Why?"

"Because that's what people do."

Aleš slipped his hand into hers. It was tougher than a shell.

"What are you doing?"

"I don't know," he said.

"Why are you holding my hand?"

"I was worried about you."

"Why?"

He squeezed tighter. "I had a bad dream."

"What happened?"

"We were on the beach together, walking into the sea, and you had both arms. And we were happy. So happy."

She let go of his hand and stepped closer, her breath hot on his cheek. "What happened next?"

"You drowned," he said, the memory straining his face.

"Drowned or *was* drowned?"

A single tear appeared in the corner of his eye. "She drowned you. This...this human crab with Zsófia's face. She whispered something to you and crabs crawled into your mouth. It was horrible."

He buried his face in his hands. Enola absorbed his sorrow with a blank stare.

"And then she pulled me under..."

"How did you know?"

"I assumed..."

"Did you ever have a dream like that?"

"About a human crab? No. It was just a stupid dream."

He hugged her. "I'm so happy that you're okay."

"Look behind you."

Aleš veered but failed to see.

"Down there, near the desk."

He intensified his gaze. Then he spotted a purple crab, crawling along the carpet.

"Is that...?"

Enola nodded. "Yes. One of her children."

"What do you mean?"

"I'm serious. She wants your heart. Be careful."

"Where are you going?" Aleš said.

"To the beach. I don't belong here, you said so yourself."

"I was joking."

She waved, then slipped out of the door.

*

The purple offspring lingered by her heel. *Click, click, click.* Its pincers performed a symphony of fury. Zsófia squatted, listening. A scowl born of anger carved into her cheeks. She offered her palm and watched it crawl along her wrist, shoulder, then inside the warm refuge of her mouth.

"Good morning."

She veered, voice raspy. "Good morning, Aleš. Was that your friend?"

"Yes. I don't think she's well."

"I think you might be right."

"Really?"

"She looks pale, malnourished."

"Okay."

"You should avoid her."

Aleš frowned. "Why?"

"She's trouble."

"Do you know her?"

"I've seen her around."

"Does she come here often?"

Zsófia sighed. "I feed her on occasion, yes."

"Feed her? Why?"

"She's destitute. You can't tell?"

"What do you mean?"

"Didn't you notice how dirty her clothes were?

Her greasy hair? Dark circles under her eyes? I think she's homeless. I feel sorry for the girl, so I feed her sometimes, you know, to make sure she gets proper...*nutrition*."

Her emphasis on the last word gave him a chill and he wondered what she meant.

"What's wrong, lad?"

"I think I'm falling in love with her."

"You barely know her," she said, chuckling.

Aleš noticed for the first time that most of her teeth were chipped. A sinister unease grew in his belly.

"I know her enough."

She leaned against the bookshelf, eyes laden with cynicism. "What do you think you *love* about her exactly?"

"Her walk..."

"Pardon?"

"She walks with this...quiet confidence. Like a warrior. Her steps are so full of purpose. And her eyes. They're fierce, wild."

"And you want to tame her, eh?"

"No," Aleš said, blushing, "but she inspires me."

"Inspires you to do what?"

"To not be afraid."

"Afraid of what?"

"The world."

"I hate to burst your bubble, lad, but she's not what you think. Love is an illusion," Zsófia said, crossing her arms.

"What do you mean?"

"You see her how you *want* to see her, not how she actually is."

"Why would you say that?"

"Because it's true. I'm older and wiser. Your heart creates an ideal image of the person. The qualities you described are just a ploy. A trick of your heart."

"My heart is playing a trick on me?"

"Yes. Your heart is pure, unscarred. Keep it that way."

"How?"

"Don't fall in love," she said.

"But that's impossible. I'm not in charge of my feelings."

Zsófia dug her nails into his shoulders. "What if you were?"

"What do you mean?"

"What if I told you, I could help you."

"Help me?"

"Not to *feel* love."

"How?"

"We just need to recondition your heart."

Enola's warning suddenly echoed in his head. *She wants your heart. She wants your heart. She wants your heart.* His mouth was desert dry. His knees quivered.

"I think I should go back now. My mum is waiting for me."

The gypsy hesitated, reluctant to soften her grip. "Of course, I don't want to get you in trouble again with my blabbering."

He wanted to smile but his muscles betrayed him.

*

Irena faffed with her bathrobe, her hair still in morning disarray. "Hey, did you find that girl?"

"Yes," Aleš said.

"Was she okay?"

He nodded.

"See? I told you it was just a dream. I got something for you. Here," she handed him a tattered bag. He pulled out a pair of navy blue rollerblades. The ball bearings rattled, wheels were misshapen, and both boot sides scuffed. A charity shop bargain, no doubt. Aleš grimaced at the embarrassing heel brake.

"Thanks, Mum."

"I know you hate that brake thing, but you can remove it."

"I know."

"There's a skatepark near the leisure centre we passed the other day. You used to enjoy skating with your friends. Thought you might want to hang out there and socialise."

"Socialise? Me?"

Irena drained her coffee cup. "This country has a way of isolating you. We can't let that happen. You had loads of friends back home. Solitude doesn't suit you. You need to communicate with kids your own age."

"I hang out with Enola all the time."

"I meant boys. You need to hang out with boys.

Play football, mess around on skates—that sort of thing."

"What's wrong with Enola?"

"Nothing's wrong with her, but she's a girl. You need boyish activities. You'll have plenty of time for girls when you're older, trust me."

"But she makes me happy, I don't *need* anybody else."

"It's not a debate," Irena said, scratching her elbow.

"Okay."

"Do you know where the skatepark is?"

"No."

"Do you remember the fountain?"

"Yeah."

"Just turn right from there. You'll see a massive green field."

"Okay."

"Do you want me to come with you?"

"No, it's fine."

"Good. Why don't you try them on and I'll make us some lunch?"

"Okay."

*

Rust infected the gate and it screeched in warning as he entered. Multiple pairs of eyeballs skated over him and Aleš instantly regretted listening to his mother. Two girls in pink tracksuits smoked on benches, while three boys rolled down a halfpipe—teasing each other with vulgar words in a pathetic showcase of male bravado. The place reeked of testosterone and raging hormones. Aleš slid onto the opposite seat, kicking off his shoes and fastening his blades.

"Heya," said the younger girl who resembled a Russian Lolita. She had a hand on her hip and her lips were painted with a provocative red. Aleš grinned, more at her thick eyebrows than her flirting attempt.

"Hello."

She took a drag of her cigarette, sucking deep, and exhaling smoke in a well-rehearsed pout.

"You new around 'ere babes?"

"Kind of," he said, eyes down and wrestling with the laces.

"What's ya name babes?"

"Aleš,"

"A whaa?"

"Aleš," he repeated.

The girls erupted with shrill laughter. "What did ya say? Alice?"

He smiled to mask his own annoyance. "Never mind."

"Aww, don't be like that babes. Lottie says you're cute and she wants to suck you off."

The other girl kicked her in the shin. "Oi. What you do da for? It's true, innit?"

One of the lads flipped 180 and rolled down the ramp backwards. He skated towards Aleš, performing the fishbrain grind along the way.

"Who da fuck is this queer?"

Aleš still fumbled with his laces, ignoring the insult. The boy was robust and older by at least four years.

"Leave him alone, Dave," Lottie said.

"Love your skates, mate. Found them in a skip? Oi. I'm talking to you."

"No, I didn't," Aleš said.

"Eh? That's a dodgy accent. You a bloody immigrant or somefink? Oi, Lottie. Your mate 'ere is a bloody immigrant."

Lottie examined her fake nails while Lolita laughed and lit another fag.

"You shouldn't be 'ere, mate. Why don't ya fuck off back to ya own country? We don't want the likes of you in Great Britain," Dave said.

"And what exactly makes *Great* Britain so great? The likes of you?" Aleš said, regretting the words almost as soon as he spoke them.

"You fucking whaa? Cheeky cunt ain't ya?"

Aleš said nothing and Dave pulled a Stanley knife from his pocket.

"Look at me, you foreign cunt. See this? I'll cut ya fucking tongue out so you can't annoy anyone else with dat minging accent."

Fear stabbed him first. Dave brushed his cheek with the tip of the blade and Aleš grew paler with each stroke.

"Are ya mental? Put da knife away, ya div," Lottie said.

Dave grinned like a serpent. "Hear that, mate? Ma

bird likes ya. What ya lookin' at her for? Wanna shag her do ya?"

The knife broke his skin. Aleš struggled with tears, but then spotted Enola. She watched from behind a shrub and pressed a finger to her lips.

"What da fuck is that?" Dave said, staring at his crotch. There was movement inside his jeans followed by a clicking sound. Dave danced a jig of panic, dropping the knife and ramming his hand down his pants.

"Lottie gave ya *crabs* or somefink?" the other girl cackled.

The double meaning amused him. Aleš grabbed his rucksack and skated out of the park, wiping drops of blood from his cheek. Enola waited around a corner, arms crossed.

"Interesting friends."

Aleš slowed down by flipping his left foot behind him and dragging the wheels sideways.

"They're not my friends, I think you know that."

"I can hurt them if you like," she said, watching him change to his trainers.

"How did you do it?"

"How did I do what?"

"The trick with the crab? How did you get it in his pants?"

Enola's face was a blank canvas. "You're still bleeding."

"It's just a scratch. Listen, thank you for saving me. I owe you one."

"Don't come here again."

"Of course not. I don't want to die just yet."

"Come with me?"

"Where?"

"Back to the hotel. I'll walk with you," she said.

"Okay."

*

The grey cobblestones mirrored his mood. Enola strode beside him in synchronised steps, her one arm stiff by her side. He glanced at the girly traffic of identical faces. Same clothes, hairstyle, make-up, mannerisms—all products of manufactured beauty. Empty, meaningless. He thought about Enola and her exquisite features. Cheekbones sharp, lips plump. Skin like porcelain.

"Are you scared still?" she said.

"No."

"What's wrong? Why won't you look at me?"

The words flew out before he could stop them. "I love you."

Enola paused, her eyes resembled two obsidian stones. "Why?"

"Because you're not like other girls," Aleš said.

"What am I like?"

"Beautiful."

"Other girls are beautiful."

"Not like you," he said.

She tilted her head. "Beauty is secondary."

"What do you mean?"

"The heart. That's what truly matters."

"The heart?"

"Or what's inside it," Enola said.

Sea breeze screamed in their ears. They strolled along the promenade hand in hand, their shoulders cloaked by mist.

"The ocean seems to change colour whenever I'm with you."

"Does it?"

He pointed. "Look, the waves are almost purple."

"Perhaps the sea is imitating our feelings."

"Why are you feeling purple?"

"I'm not. You are."

"No, I'm not."

"Watch this," Enola said, pressing her lips to his. When she kissed him, the colour of the sea mutated instantly. It now glowed with a dark shade of purple. Aleš forgot how to breathe. The soft grace of her lips induced a temporary coma.

"Have a look," she said.

Aleš blinked and faced the ocean. "Whoa. How did you do that?"

"Your heart did it."

"What do you mean?"

"Hearts are like diamonds to me."

He frowned. "I still don't get it."

"The sea responds to you. The purer the heart, the darker the water."

"I always thought red was the colour of love."

"Maybe purple is the colour of passion," Enola said, peering into the waves.

"My heart must be pretty pure then. That water is seriously murky."

"Yes, the darkest I've seen. Your heart is loyal but delicate. If broken, you'll die."

"What?"

"Invest your feelings with care is all I'm saying."

"Okay. Any tips for the future?"

Enola faced him, sweeping black curls behind her ears. "Have you ever heard of the Crabian Heart?"

"No. What is that?"

"I have one. It protects me."

"Protects you from what?"

"Inevitable heartaches."

Aleš processed her words. "Why did you kiss me?"

"To show you."

"Not because you like me?"

"I do like you."

"Okay. Why did you help me in the skatepark?"

"I don't know," she said.

"Because you like me?"

"Yes."

"Is it true that you're homeless?"

Enola paused by a lonely bench.

"Why are you stopping?" Aleš said.

"My joints hurt. I need to sit down."

"Okay."

"Who told you I was homeless?"

"Zsófia," he said, sitting down next to her.

The name angered her. "She's just speculating."

"But she said she feeds you?"

"She feeds me crabs sometimes, yes."

"Crabs?"

Enola nodded.

"What do they taste like?"

"Like something out of this world."

Aleš held her hand. "Mum said they'll move us soon."

"Who?"

"The immigration people."

"Why?"

"The hotel is just a temporary solution."

"When?"

"I don't know, but I'm scared."

She gazed at him. "Of what?"

"Of losing you. What's the matter?"

"My jaw is stiff. It hurts when I speak."

They swam in each other's eyes, but her unconventional beauty began to drown him.

"Do you want me to kiss you again?"

"Okay," he said, pouting his lips.

*

Someone slurped in the kitchenette. Aleš crept over the threshold, gazing at the gypsy's hands. They were busy in the sink. He ventured closer, only to lose balance. A faint spell possessed him. The basin was full of hearts. Instead of fingers, she had pincers. A giant set of pincers, tearing hearts apart with visible hatred.

"Jesus," he said.

Zsófia veered, her nostrils flaring and chunks of raw meat trapped between her chipped teeth. Blood leaked from the still-pumping heart in her pincers and her lips were painted dark red.

"That's what makes you weak, lad. Your heart."

"What?"

"Give it to me or she'll break it."

Aleš retreated when she pointed at his chest.

"Did you hear? I said give it to me."

"B-but it's my *heart*. I need it to live," he said, stuttering.

"No, you need it to *feel*. She wants you for herself. Let me help you before it's too late."

"Help me how?"

Zsófia regurgitated a crab, dressed in purple slime. She seized the crustacean in her pincer and offered him to Aleš.

"Eat."

The boy shook his head.

"Do you know what love is?"

Aleš shrugged his shoulders this time.

"A slow poison."

"I don't understand…"

"She's poisoning your heart already, but there's still time."

"Time for what?"

"To escape the pain," Zsófia said.

"But I'm not in pain…"

"Not yet. Love poisons us all, but a cure exists."

"What cure?"

She pointed at her own chest. "The Crabian Heart. I can give it to you."

"How?"

"Eat."

"Did Enola eat your crabs, too?"

The gypsy cackled. "You silly boy. She is the Mother of Crabs."

"What do you mean?"

She shifted to the sink and began to pummel him with raptured hearts. Aleš shielded his face, but organs still slapped him from both sides.

"They're all useless. Scarred. Broken."

"Please, stop."

The onslaught ceased, and he dared to open an eye. Zsófia kneeled, her pincer caressing his cheek.

"Your heart is still pure and she wants it."

"Why?"

Zsófia grinned. "Let me show you."

She ripped his clothes off with her pincers and Aleš screamed.

"Calm down, lad. What's the matter with you?"

He blinked, frantic. Zsófia pulled him up, her hands human again.

"What happened?"

"I think you had a minor shock when you saw the hearts."

"So it was real?"

"What was?"

"The sink was filled with hearts and you had

pincers instead of hands. You wanted my heart and ripped it out of my chest."

She rolled her eyes. "Have you been sniffing glue, lad? That's not good for you. You're hallucinating."

"But it seemed so real…"

"The sink is full of hearts, yes. Pig hearts. A true delicacy."

Bile tickled his throat. "That's disgusting."

"They don't look appetising, I admit, but they're an aphrodisiac once cooked."

"A what?"

"Never mind. I'm having some of my Hungarian relatives over for dinner. You want to give me a hand?"

"Eww. No."

"How about your heart?" she said, poking him in the chest.

The boy winced.

"I'm only joking, silly. You want a cup of tea? Look at you—you're shaking."

"I'm okay. It's just…you were a monster."

The gypsy raised a brow. "We're all monsters, lad. You sure? Want some food instead?"

"No, I'm good. Have a nice evening and enjoy your…meal."

"Oh, we certainly will. You don't know what you're missing."

"I think I do," he said.

"If you say so. Give my regards to your mother."

"Okay."

Aleš turned on his heel and bolted up the stairs.

In their room, Irena was drowning in a sea of paperwork. He hung his rucksack on the chair.

"Hey. Did you find the skatepark?"

"Um-hum."

"Decent ramps?"

"I didn't really try them," Aleš said.

She looked up. "Why not?"

"It was just packed."

"Okay, made any new friends?"

"New enemies more like."

Irena tossed a heap of papers aside. "What?"

"I don't wanna talk about it."

"Come here, sit down."

Then she spotted the cut on his cheek.

"What happened? Did you get into a fight?"

Aleš recoiled when she touched him.

"It's just a tiny cut, I'll be fine."

"Tell me what happened. Right now."

"Fine," he sighed, "I got there and some girl asked my name."

"And?"

"I opened my mouth and it was over."

Irena rolled her eyes. "You're not making any sense. What did you say?"

"That's the whole point. It's not about what I said."

"What's it about then?"

"What I *sounded* like."

"You sound normal to me."

"To you, but not to them. We don't belong here, Mum."

Her mind raced, interpreting half-truths and hidden meanings.

"Is that what they said? That you don't belong here? Because you're a foreigner?"

Aleš averted his gaze. "Something like that."

"You shouldn't listen to those cretins."

"But what if they're right? I don't feel like I belong here. Do you?"

"You will in time," Irena said.

"But what if I still feel the same in twenty years?"

"If shit tasted like sugar, I'd put it in my coffee. Life is too short to worry about ifs."

"Okay."

She gripped his shoulder. "In life, you'll encounter all sorts of people. Good and bad. No matter where you live. No matter where you go. We're not extra-terrestrials just because we speak a different language. We're still human beings, made of flesh and blood. Forget about those nincompoops. Good-hearted folks still exist. You just have to find them."

"Good-hearted?"

"You know, someone with a good heart?"

"I have a good heart," Aleš said.

"No, darling. You have an *exceptional* heart."

*

The ocean had no memory. He perched on a solitary boulder and imagined life without love.

His childish mind failed to grasp the possibility. Zsófia was a bitter old woman. Why should he judge romance based on her experiences alone?

"Hey. What are you thinking about?"

He glanced below and saw Enola. Her hair was dyed purple.

"What have you done to your hair?"

"You don't like it?"

"I do, looks nice."

Enola wrapped a curl of hair around her finger. "What are you thinking about?"

"Love."

She narrowed her eyes. "And what do you know about love?"

"I know I love *you*," Aleš said, but his voice lacked conviction.

"But?"

"But it's just something Zsófia said."

"What did she say?"

He rubbed his palm. "That you will break my heart."

"Heart-breaks are inevitable. If I don't break your heart, someone else will."

A seagull cried in the distance.

"So that's it? There's no hope?"

"No hope, but a solution. The Crabian Heart."

"But I don't want it. I want love. I want to *feel* love. When I wake up in the morning, I think about your face. When I close my eyes at night, I think about your kisses. *You* are my hope. You are my *heart*."

"And if your love is misplaced?" Enola said.

"I don't think it is."

"Hmm."

"Why did she call you Mother of Crabs?"

Enola's face melted into a painful smile. "That's what people call me around here. I like crabs, but I'm not their mother. That's silly."

"Why do you like crabs so much?"

"They're my friends."

"But you warned me to stay away from them," he said.

"Yes, they're not for you."

"Why?"

"As I said, they are not what they seem."

"Why aren't you at school?"

"Summer holidays…"

"Oh."

She climbed onto the boulder next to him, but her movements were slow and arduous.

"You okay?"

"Yes, just not very flexible."

"You're a kid. Every kid is flexible."

"I'm…different."

"I know."

Aleš kissed her and she let him.

"Do you want to feel my breast?"

He hesitated. "No, it's okay. I just like being with you."

"How far have you gone with a girl?"

"What do you mean?"

"Sexually," Enola said.

"Erm, you're my first."

"I'm honoured. So just a kiss?"

Aleš nodded, cheeks warm with embarrassment. "Have you been with other boys?"

"Yes."

His stomach knotted with something like jealousy. "Okay."

"Are you angry with me?"

"No," he lied.

"Does your heart ache?"

"A little. Why?"

"This is your first lesson," she said.

"Lesson in what?"

Enola stroked his cheek and her fingers smelled like seaweed.

"When it comes to love, you'll always end up disappointed."

"I'm not disappointed."

"Of course you are. Your face burns with anger."

"No, it doesn't."

"What if I told you that other boys touched me? That I touched them?"

"Why are you telling me this?"

Enola leaned closer. "How they caressed my breasts, kissed my lips…"

"Stop it."

"Your heart aches with every word, I can *feel* it."

Tears broke free and he leapt into the pebbles. "Leave me alone, you crippled whore. I don't ever want to see you again, you hear me?"

*

Aleš sprinted along the darkening promenade. His heart screamed like it was flooded with acid. The bitter taste of despair burned on his tongue.

Cars honked as he darted across the road, driven by senseless fury. Life or death seemed relevant no longer. Only her. She was the centre of his wounded heart.

"What happened to you?" Irena said when he burst through the door, panting and leaking perspiration.

"She betrayed me."

"Who?"

He bent over like a human straw, slurping oxygen. "Enola."

"That girl from the beach?"

Aleš nodded, drops of sweat staining the carpet.

"How did she betray you?"

"She...she allowed other boys to touch her."

Irena's forehead wrinkled with worry. "Was she your girlfriend then?"

"I don't know."

"If she had other boyfriends in the past that's normal, you know?"

"I thought she was mine," Aleš said.

"I understand your confusion, but she's not an object. She doesn't belong to you."

"But I love her. I wanted her for myself."

Irena inhaled, desperately brewing wisdom for her son. "It won't make much sense now, but you'll have other girlfriends, too."

"I don't want other girlfriends. Only her."

"We can't always have who we want. It's called unrequited love."

"I don't care what it's called. She's fickle."

"Many women are. I'm sorry, darling, but it's for the best. Listen, come here."

He sat on the bed where Irena pointed.

"I know this isn't the ideal time, but we have bigger problems."

"What problems?"

She sighed. "Our asylum claim was denied."

"And?"

"It means we lost."

"So?"

"So they're going to deport us."

His brain quaked and the room shrunk. Enola. He would not see her again and the thought nauseated him.

"Don't cry, we'll be okay."

"But I have to apologise to her. I was mean and horrible."

Irena embraced her son. "Another time. Stay here, we have to start packing."

"When will they come for us?"

"I don't know, but soon I imagine."

"What about Dad?"

"He was deported yesterday. We're next."

He sprang to his feet. "I have to see her *now*. I can't leave like this."

"It'll take a few days at least. There's no need to hurry. You barely know this girl."

"But she saved me."

"Saved you? From who? What are you talking about?"

"The kids at the skatepark. I owe her."

Irena massaged her temples. "Why don't you bring her here? I'd like to meet her."

"Why?"

"I want to see the girl that captured my son's heart."

"Okay, but she's shy and probably hates me now."

"There's a bar of chocolate in the cupboard. Women love chocolate."

"Everyone loves chocolate."

"Yes, but women especially."

"Okay."

Irena grinned. "Good boy. Give her the chocolate, apologise, and bring her to me."

*

The gypsy tested her luck on the fruit machine. She waved but his mind was distracted. It ploughed words of regret, love, and comfort. He mumbled, rehearsing apologetic phrases over and over.

"Where you off to?"

His nails sunk into the melting chocolate bar in his hand. "I have to find Enola."

"At this hour? It's dark and cold outside," she said, pressing buttons.

"We had a fight. I have to apologise."

"You can apologise in the morning…"

"It might be too late. Mum said they'll deport us."

She licked her chipped teeth. "Yes, I've heard. I'm sorry, lad. It's a terrible thing."

"What is?"

"The system," Zsófia said, shifting her gaze back to the slot machine, "is a gamble, you know? A lottery. Some people get lucky, some don't."

"Okay."

"My advice is that you should forget her. She won't be part of your life for much longer."

"But I can't leave on bad terms. I have to make things right."

"I told you, she's bad news. Leave her alone. You'll be out of her reach soon."

"I can't. I love her."

Zsófia nodded towards the kitchen. "Come with me. I want to show you something."

"But I have to go…"

"I'll be quick, promise."

"Okay."

He followed her into a spacious prep area that reeked of fish.

"Behind that curtain, take a look."

Aleš brushed it aside, peering. "I can't see anything."

"Look closer."

A sharp blow turned his world to black.

The rope irritated his bare skin. Aleš wiggled on the floor, topless and impotent. His hair was matted with dry blood. She kneeled over him, pressing her palm on his chest and counting beats.

"Your heart is so ripe,"

Aleš whimpered. "Why are you hurting me?"

"Hurting you? No, lad. I'm *protecting* you. You'll thank me when it's over."

"When what is over?"

Her jaw cracked. "Your heart. I must preserve it."

"Please don't eat my heart."

Purple marks stained his skin when she lifted her fingers. "Stay still now."

"My mum expects me within the hour. You won't get away with this."

"Your mother is irrelevant. She can't have you."

"But she's my mother," he pleaded.

"I'm not talking about your mother. Be silent or—"

A giant pincer punctured her back with a roaring crunch, ripping out her heart. Zsófia's eyes bulged and a pool of viscera formed beneath her feet. The boy gasped, drinking in the sight of his saviour through the massive hole in Zsófia's chest. Enola's face beamed at him. Her left arm transformed into a pincer and clutching the gypsy's still beating heart. She ogled it with disgust.

"Help me, Enola. Please, help me. She wanted to kill me."

Enola tossed the heart aside and stepped closer. She snipped the rope with her pincer and Aleš threw his arms around her neck.

"I'm so sorry for what I said earlier. I was angry. I didn't mean it. I love you so much. I love you, I love you with all my heart."

Enola blinked, unresisting. "Look at me. I'm a freak."

"I don't care."

"You're not repulsed?"

"No," he said, squeezing tighter.

"I'm not right for you. I'm a monster."

"You're not a monster. You're my heart. I love you."

"But I'm a heartbreaker, that's what I do. That's what I *love*."

"What do you mean?"

"I break hearts."

He let go. "And what makes my heart so special?"

"You feel pain others can't."

"They're going to deport me."

"When?"

"Soon. My mother wants to meet you."

"Why?"

Aleš rubbed his chest. "To thank you for helping me at the skatepark, I think."

"There's no time. We must go."

"Go where?"

"To the beach," she said.

"Now? It's late."

"Do you want to be with me or not?"

"You know I do."

"Then trust me."

"Okay."

*

They strolled along the shore. Enola stopped, her face even paler in the moonlight.

"Humans are born alone and they die alone. Don't you think that's sad?"

"I never really thought about it," Aleš said.

She slipped out of her shoes. "Come with me."

"Where?"

"Into the midnight sea."

"Don't be silly, it's freezing."

Enola plodded into the purple waves, her legs swallowed by the ocean. "Come to me."

"You're crazy. Hold on."

He removed his own trainers and followed her.

"What if I told you there was a way for us to be together. Always."

"How? Can you grant me asylum?"

Enola kissed him. "Even better, I can grant you eternal life. In a way."

"What do you mean?"

She opened her mouth and legions of small crustaceans crawled out. Aleš gasped, losing balance in the water. Crabs marched down her chest, slowly engulfing her entire body.

"What are they?"

"My slaves," Enola said, "all the boys and men

who fell in love with me. I broke their hearts."

"But they're crabs!"

"Yes, and I am their mother now."

"What have you done to them?"

"I offered the Crabian Heart and they accepted. Now they are bound to me for all eternity. They feel what I feel. I love them all."

"But you don't love me?"

"I can't love you. Not unless you become part of the family."

Aleš dunked his head beneath the waves, trying to drown his confusion. "There is no other way?"

"You can still refuse. But now you're finally beginning to understand that love is a plague. Cruel and torturous. You can leave right now and be deported tomorrow or the day after. I won't stop you. In time, I'll fade from your memory. You will love again. You will hate again. The cycle continues until you die. Alone. Or you can stay and accept my gift. You can vanish from this world and never be seen or hurt again. You can be with me always."

"You want me to be your slave, is that it?"

"Aren't we all slaves when it comes to love?"

She pinched a purple crab from her hair and dangled it over his mouth. "The choice is yours."

FOUNTAIN OF DROWNED MEMORIES

Lorcan's blurry gaze collided with the stains. He studied them with utter fright—these blotches, sifting through the ceiling and invading his privacy. When did they appear? And for what purpose? Lorcan failed to remember. His mind was an abyss of extinct memories. With each passing day his thoughts faded into nothing, never to be salvaged.

A faint light penetrated the room, casting shadows over the stains that tormented his mind. The mattress reeked of urine and Lorcan pinched his nose—peering at the warped patterns. He groaned at its revolting finish. An ugly texture—like virginal flesh tarnished with scars.

The room felt chilly and unfamiliar. Where was he? The old man's eyes returned to the ceiling. That feckin' material, what yer call it? Why can't I remember? He chased the word through the dim labyrinth of his brain, but it proved elusive—a recurring race he failed to win.

Lorcan nipped into the creased knuckle of his index finger, frustrated but still determined.

The word lingered on the tip of his tongue—he could almost taste it. Plaster! That's it.

Plaster. An accomplished grin spread across his

pigmented features. These little victories resurrected his motivation.

Tossing the quilt aside, Lorcan idled on the bed — examining the varicose veins on his shin with dismay. The purple veins seemed to be wriggling — like worms beneath his skin. When did they appear? He failed to remember that, too. Lorcan quivered at the traumatising prospect of losing himself completely — feebly moaning in despair, rocking back and forth. It changed him. The face in the mirror did not belong to him. This thing consumed emotions, thoughts and desires — leaving behind nothing but a bleak trail of emptiness.

The corroded tap unleashed a single drop of water that collided with the sink and disturbed his surreal nightmare.

Lorcan shifted his gaze towards the source of the sound, listening. The tranquil drip calmed what remained of his fragile mind. The word 'sink' had vanished from his memory ages ago so he called it a fountain instead.

The cabalistic fountain summoned him now.

Lorcan's knees protested with a clamorous crack as he limped, steps full of uncertainty — like a toddler beginning to walk. Leaning on the edges, he glared into the chrome drain and the chasm beyond. He uncoiled the plug and filled the fountain with tepid water. Heal me again, please. Wash it away. I beg ya.

Euphoria sponged his brain as he submerged, bubbles erupting. The fountain massaged his emotions, filtering and banishing negative thoughts. He felt the mysterious power healing him. Anxiety and confusion retreated. Dirty memories bathed clean — then drowned beneath the surface.

Lorcan's soaked head emerged from the fountain, his toothless mouth gasping for air. Revitalised, he dried the strands of his pewter-coloured hair with an embroidered towel which he found draped around a dusty chair. The fountain produced miracles and he felt like a restored ruin. It granted clarity, if only for a while. The black cloud that devoured his identity halted. Such was the divine faculty of the fountain. He glanced upwards, at the stains.

They seemed inky, more prominent — as if they'd absorbed whatever the fountain had sucked out of him. Are they connected? The fountain and the stains?

The ceiling quaked and Lorcan staggered. A fusion of stomping and vicious laughter ensued from above.

Disoriented, he approached the window. The condensation on the surface of the glass reminded him of tears and he broke into a sob because of it — a catastrophic reaction. He smudged the condensation aside, the moisture soaking into his palms. The view invoked further melancholy. A grey mist sprinkled dew on the grass and the distorted figures of strangers briskly faded out of sight — into the fog, into nothing.

Who are these people? He mused over the stark landscape with an empty heart, cursing the limited visibility. Lorcan struggled to recall the life that once existed outside of these walls. How long have I been here? Outlines of trees swayed somewhere in the distance but where was the breeze, he wondered? Silence dominated all. Then it dawned on him. The window! I cannot hear the wind because of the window. Who put it there? His fist pounded on the glass, eager to shatter the barrier that obstructed his reality.

"Mr Carmody? What's the matter?" said a gentle voice he did not recognize. He veered around, wary and frightened. A slender woman flashed a smile, her teeth stained from years of tea drinking.

"Why are yer tormenting me? Are yer the stain-master?" Lorcan said, noticing that her teeth
and the ceiling stains shared an identical shade of brown. Did it consume her too? Gnawing from within? Or was she a messenger? The stain-master disguised in a female form?

"I've been called a lot of things in my life, but never a stain-master — whatever that is. You need to sit down and stop banging on the window, Mr Carmody. You're disturbing the others and you'll hurt yourself. Now we don't want that, do we?"

He refused to listen. "Get away from me, yer gowl. Fer weeks, yer been drugging me. Don't ya dare shake yer head at me. It won't work. Yer cannot change me. The fountain heals everything, yer hear me?"

The woman stepped back, hands raised in peace. She scowled at the whiff of urine. "Mr Carmody, please calm down. I'll bring you your breakfast and I'll change the sheets for you. We don't want you to marinate in that, do we?"

"Yer'd like that, wouldn't ya? Eh? Keep me alive so yer can torture me some more."

Defeated, she shut the door behind her with an amiable force while Lorcan continued barking threats.

"It's getting worse. I'm not sure how much longer we have before it consumes him entirely,"
she said to the man waiting outside.

*

He crossed the room, nodding and mumbling curses. That manky whore. Acting like a mentaller. Off 'er nut she is.

The soles of Lorcan's slippers squeaked as he dragged them across the linoleum.

Who was she? Where had he seen that ugly mug before? The fountain gurgled. He winced, shoulders tense. Yer know, don't ya? Hunching over the sink, Lorcan inhaled. It reeked of rotten eggs and he coughed. The ceiling stains gathered like distant clouds of impending doom. Drops of water escaped from the faucet. Drip drip. He blinked, feeling drowsy. The serene sound relaxed his limbs. Sleep beckoned. Black liquid suddenly flowed from the drain, filling and rising to the brim. Lorcan gasped, his senses bursting to life. Hesitating, he dipped his tongue into it—sampling, savouring. The flavour revitalised him instantly. He soaked his entire face, gulping and slurping—the liquid dribbling down his stubby chin. This tastes like Guinness! It reminded him of the old days when he was getting langered in the pubs of Clonakilty.

I remembered! Lorcan probed in his mind, searching like a greedy hand in a pocket full of holes. Nothing. The fountain offered no more.

Why is this happening? Why can't I remember who I am? Where I am? Or why I'm here?

The void frightened him. He trembled, paranoia gnawing at his core and once again—Lorcan questioned his identity.

I'm Lorcan...but who is Lorcan? I don't know anything about him. About meself. Is this really me? I'm so confused...

The fountain squirted more black liquid, commanding him to drink, and drink he did, deeply—like a baby hungry for its mother's milk. He fell to his knees, drunk on illusions.

A mouth appeared at the base of the fountain, its lips mushy and plump. It spoke, uttering Gaelic words he failed to comprehend. A slimy black tongue appeared also, stretching toward the ceiling—transforming into a tentacle, slithering with floating memories. Lorcan rubbed his eyes in a faint attempt to banish the hallucination. The tentacle injected fluid into the ceiling and the stains multiplied. He blinked, observing in silent terror—piecing together fragments of his broken mind. It occurred to Lorcan, that somehow the fountain drained his memories. The legion of brown stains expanded. Did they represent memories? His memories? Stolen by the fountain? For what purpose? But the fountain had promised to restore his memory, enhance it—to save him from the evolving nothingness. He felt robbed, betrayed. The tentacle retreated, brushing his kneecap. Lorcan quivered in shock, grimacing at the stranded slime. So putrid.

"Mr Carmody, why are you sitting on the cold floor? Are you alright?" said the woman.

Lorcan failed to acknowledge her presence. She stepped closer, her voice tender. "Mr Carmody? Can you hear me?"

He nodded. "It betrayed me...the fountain. It betrayed me..."

"Let me help. Here, hold my hand, Mr Carmody," she said, offering her robust arm. "Here we go. See? That wasn't so bad, was it?"

The woman guided Lorcan back to bed.

"It betrayed me...the fountain. It betrayed me..."

"Yes, I heard you the first time. Everything will be alright. Take these pills for me, Mr Carmody, they'll help you sleep."

Lorcan blinked, his accusing eyes shifting from the drugs to the woman's sly grin. "Hump off. I don't wanna take them feckin' pills."

"But you need rest, Mr Carmody. You'll feel better, trust me."

"Hump off. I don't wanna take them feckin' pills," he repeated.

"Please, don't be stubborn, Mr Carmody."

"I'm not Mr Carmody…"

The woman sighed with defeat. "Then who are you?"

"I don't know, do I?"

*

The mouth-watering aroma of bacon stirred him. Lorcan groaned, eyeing the steaming plate with suspicion. He recognised the smell, but not the meat. Who put it there, on the tray, next to his bed? Why didn't he hear them come in? Senses. Now it drowned his senses, too. The ceiling cracked again and he gasped as he observed the texture.

The plaster was replaced with human skin. Scarred, wrinkly old skin. His skin? Lorcan glanced at his hands, half-scared to discover flesh and bone.

If he angered the fountain, would it seek revenge by skinning him alive? His hands throbbed but remained the same. He studied the chart of veins. How much he loathed veins. Biology made Lorcan queasy.

He picked up the plate and sliced off a rasher of bacon. He bit into it with toothless gums, toughened by years of repetition. It tasted vile—like rubber engulfed in salt. Lorcan chewed, eyes glued to the ceiling. He tried to swallow but forgot how—the reflex refused to obey.

Then he noticed it. When he sliced into the meat,

a similar cut appeared in the ceiling. In the brown, skin-like plaster. Lorcan spat it out. Sustenance no longer mattered. Why should it when he was trapped in this madness, fading with each passing day? He felt so alone, abandoned, sacrificed. For a time, he had believed that the fountain would cure him, stop the process—rescue him from the advancing nothingness. Now he doubted its capabilities. What did it crave? Truly? Did it prey on his memories? On his very essence? Today, he would stay in bed. Rest.

The fountain bewitched him with its promises of restoration—offering to return Lorcan to his former self. Lies. All lies. His hands began to tremor again. Then he felt the pressure in his...bladder? Was that the right word?

Yes, yes, bladder. That's it. I really need to use the jacks before I piss meself, he thought.

When Lorcan stopped resisting, the warm urine flowed down his thigh. It stank, as if he solely existed on an asparagus diet. Wriggling his nose, he failed to remember where the toilet was. Delirium swallowed him. What had he become? The fountain whispered but he ignored the feeble calls. Instead of replenishing his memories, it drowned them. He accepted that now.

Raindrops began to collide with the window. Against the protests of his bones, Lorcan limped forth. The drops formed a map on the surface.

He traced the passage with his fingertips, memorising the route then crying in frustration.

Memorising. That ability perished long ago. Why was nothing sinking in? Why was he cursed with this eternal nothingness? Devoid of logic, emotion, action—unable to think for himself. His identity stripped, discarded, consumed by this barren wasteland.

The sky outside turned onyx, overshadowing everything. Trees, grass, birds, clouds—they all disappeared. For a moment, he wondered if it mirrored his stagnant brain. Once again, he glanced at the fountain. It orchestrated all of this. Lorcan was sure of it. With all his might, he picked up the chair and raised it overhead—aiming at the deceitful instrument of evil.

"Mr Carmody! What on earth are you doing? Put the chair down right now, before you hurt yourself," said the voice he still failed to recognise.

"Who are yer? Do I know ya?" Lorcan said, lowering the chair.

"Of course you do. I'm Caitlin. I'm taking care of you. Remember?"

"Eh?"

"I'm Caitlin. You remember me, don't you?" she repeated.

He frowned. The woman's plump figure began to warp. Her voice fading, like she called to him from afar—yet she stood right there in front of him. Was this another trick of the fountain?

"How are you feeling, Mr Carmody?"

Lorcan snivelled, attempting to decipher the simple question and the hidden meaning behind it.

"Stop acting the maggot, Katherine. Who are yer really? What are yer doing to me?"

She approached him then, but Lorcan recoiled.

"Please sit down, Mr Carmody."

"Eh? Sit?" he said.

"Yes, sit down—there on the bed," Caitlin pointed.

"I...don't know how."

"Here, let me show you."

She guided Lorcan to the edge of the mattress, helping him sit on a dry patch.

"I did it all arseways, I'm banjaxed..." he mumbled.

"It's okay, Mr Carmody. There's someone here to see you."

"Eh? I'm in no mood for bogtrotters. I need me some black stuff."

"We can't allow you to drink, Mr Carmody, you know that."

"Yer cheesing me off, lassie. I'm gonna clatter ya." Lorcan raised his arm in a striking motion but it remained limp by his side.

"Just sit tight, Mr Carmody, and I'll bring him in."

He struggled to register Caitlin's hollow words. The temperature dropped and Lorcan's gums chattered. A few drops of water escaped from the faucet. The fountain stirred, tempting him to step closer once again. Seduced, he tried to stand but his knees buckled.

It gurgled a hungry echo. The sound bounced off the

walls and Lorcan covered his ears. Then he felt sturdy fingers grip his shoulder. Lorcan shrieked in horror.

"Dad? It's okay. It's Donal, your son…"

Panting, Lorcan glared at the man before him — wide-eyed.

"Lay off, yer gobshite. Who are ya? Another one of fountain's creatures? Are yer the stain master? Yer are, aren't ya? Eh?"

Donal remained silent, pondering Caitlin's earlier words to him. She was right. It had spread.

He didn't even recognise his own son. It consumed him and there was nothing he could do…

"Whatcha lookin' at, boyo? Eh? Who are ya?"

"I'm your son, Donal. Don't you recognise me?" he said.

Lorcan's mouth stiffened. "Me son? Are yer gone in the 'ead?"

"I am your son — your only son. Don't you remember me?"

He lowered his gaze. "I…the fountain drowned me memories. I don't remember ya, Son."

Donal frowned, flushed with sympathy. "The fountain? What are you talking about, Dad?"

Drip drip. "It knows, Son. It knows we're talking about it. I… I can't…"

"It's alright. I'm here for you, Dad. What do you mean by the fountain?"

Lorcan lubricated his throat, raising a wrinkly finger — pointing at it.

"The sink? What about it?" Donal said.

"Shhhh, yer plonker. It'll hear ya," Lorcan said, pressing a finger to his cracked lips.

In comfort, Donal reached for his father's trembling hand. "Dad, it's just a sink. It won't hurt you."

Lorcan blinked with a vacuous expression. "Yer don't understand. The fountain drowned me memories. It's got tentacles. Slimy tentacles. They got memories fixed to them. My memories! It's erasing them, don't yer see? It...it injects them into the ceiling—look."

Donal raised his eyes, peering at the ceiling. "The stains? They're just water stains, Dad. Probably from a leaky roof. You have nothing to worry about."

"Nothing? That's exactly it, yer sap. Nothing. I live with nothing. My mind's turned to shite. Consumed by nothing. I don't remember nothing. NOTHING! The fountain drowned me memories," Lorcan yelled.

"Dad, calm down. I have to tell you some-thing. Please, sit down."

Exhaustion forced him to obey. The old man sat down, listening.

Donal sighed. "Dad, the sink—the fountain— didn't drown your memories."

"Eh? What yer on about, boyo?"

"You're ill and confused. You have dementia," Donal said, gently.

Lorcan frowned, the meaning of the word wasted on him. "But the stains...the fountain...the tentacles..."

"Memory loss, hallucinations, confusion, tremors, loss of appetite—it's all connected with dementia, Dad."

Stubborn as ever, Lorcan waved his hand. "Dirty nonsense. Scram, yer bastard. Yer ain't no son of mine."

A tear trickled down Donal's cheek and he crushed it with a knuckle. They had told him what to expect, yet he struggled to see his father in such a vulnerable state. What could he do?

"It's okay, Dad. I'll stay with you. No one will hurt you, I promise."

Lorcan shivered. "Eh? What were we talking about?"

"That I'll stay with you, protect you."

The old man smiled for the first time in ages. "From the fountain?"

"Yes, Dad—from the fountain."

The sink gurgled. Both men turned their heads toward the sound.

ABOUT THE AUTHOR

Erik Hofstatter is a dark fiction writer and a member of the Horror Writers Association. Born in the wild lands of the Czech Republic, he roamed Europe before subsequently settling on English shores, studying creative writing at the London School of Journalism. He now dwells in Kent, where he can be encountered consuming copious amounts of mead and tyrannizing local peasantry. His work appeared in various magazines and podcasts around the world such as *Morpheus Tales, Crystal Lake Publishing, The Literary*

Hatchet, Sanitarium Magazine, Wicked Library, Tales to Terrify and *Manor House Show*. Other works include *The Pariahs, Amaranthine and Other Stories, Katerina, Moribund Tales* and *Rare Breeds*.

www.erikhofstatter.net

Twitter: @ErikHofstatter

Facebook: *www.facebook.com/erikhofstatter*

Also available:

RADIX OMNIUM MALUM by Mike Chinn
ISBN: 978-0-9957173-0-5

SHADES by Joseph Rubas
ISBN: 978-0-9935742-9-0

THE CHAMELEON MAN by David Williamson
ISBN: 978-0-9935742-9-3

A PLACE OF SKULLS by David Ludford
ISBN: 978-0-9935742-6-9

HAUNTED GRAVE by Ezeiyoke Chukwunonso
ISBN: 978-0-9935742-3-8

INTO THE DARK by Andrew Jennings
ISBN: 978-0-9935742-5-2

TOUGH GUYS by Adrian Cole
ISBN: 978-0-9935742-2-1

CLASSIC WEIRD 2 selected by David A. Riley
ISBN: 978-0-9932888-4-5

OTHER VISIONS OF HEAVEN AND HELL by Jessica Palmer
ISBN: 978-0-9935742-1-4

A SAUCERFUL OF SECRETS by Andrew Darlington
ISBN: 978-0-9935742-0-7

THE WINTER HUNT AND OTHER STORIES
by Steve Lockley & Paul Lewis
ISBN: 978-0-9932888-9-0

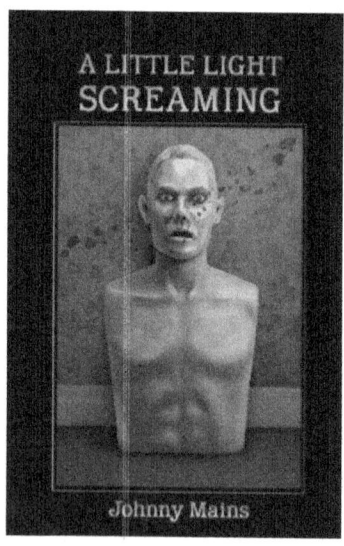

A LITTLE LIGHT SCREAMING by Johnny Mains
ISBN: 978-0-9932888-5-2

ENGLAND 'B': 90 MINUTES OF HELL by Richard Staines
ISBN: 978-0-9932888-7-6

AND NOBODY LIVED HAPPILY EVER AFTER by Kate Farrell
ISBN: 978-0-9932888-8-3

FISHHEAD: THE DARKER TALES OF IRVIN S. COBB
ISBN: 978-0-9935742-4-5

KITCHEN SINK GOTHIC: Selected by David and Linden Riley
ISBN: 978-0-9932888-3-8

MOLOCH'S CHILDREN by David A. Riley
ISBN: 978-0-9932888-1-4

STANDING ON THE THRESHOLD OF MADNESS
by Benjamin Blake
ISBN: 978-0-9957173-1-2

Check our website

paralleluniversepublications.blogspot.co.uk/

tained

33B/144/P